MAY 2011

EDGE BOOKS

WARRIORS OF HISTORY

MONGOL WARRIORS

by Terri Dougherty

Consultant:
Haomin Gong
East Asian Languages and Cultures and
Comparative Literature
University of California, Davis

Capstone
press

Mankato, Minnesota

Edge Books are published by Capstone Press,
151 Good Counsel Drive, P.O. Box 669, Mankato, Minnesota 56002.
www.capstonepress.com

Library of Congress Cataloging-in-Publication Data
Dougherty, Terri.
    Mongol warriors. / by Terri Dougherty.
    p. cm. — (Edge books. Warriors of history)
    Includes bibliographical references and index.
    ISBN-13: 978-1-4296-1312-5 (hardcover)
    ISBN-10: 1-4296-1312-2 (hardcover)
    1. Mongols — History — Juvenile literature. 2. Military art and
science — Mongolia — History — To 1500 — Juvenile literature. I. Title. II. Series.
DS19.S537 2008
950'.2 — dc22   2007029962

Summary: Describes the life of a Mongol warrior, including his training, weapons,
    and what led to the downfall of his society.

Editorial Credits
Mandy Robbins, editor; Thomas Emery, set designer; Kyle Grenz, book designer;
    Jo Miller, photo researcher; Tod Smith, illustrator; Krista Ward, colorist

Photo Credits
Alamy/North Wind Picture Archives, 8–9; Visual Arts Library (London), 17, 18
Corbis/Barry Lewis, cover; Bettmann 26
Getty Images Inc./Jean-Marc Giboux, 28; National Geographic/James L. Stanfield,
    14; The Bridgeman Art Library, 12; Time Life Pictures/Mansell, 7
The Granger Collection, New York, 23
Mary Evans Picture Library, 4, 11, 24, 27

1 2 3 4 5 6 13 12 11 10 09 08

TABLE OF CONTENTS

CHAPTER 1
BUILDING AN EMPIRE

LEARN ABOUT:

- A surprise attack
- United warriors
- Terror on horseback

Mongol attacks were sudden and brutal.

In March 1220, the citizens of Bukhara in central Asia felt safe behind their city's walls. The city's leader, the Shah, thought he knew where the enemy Mongol forces were gathered. But Mongol leader Genghis Khan and his army appeared on horseback just outside the city. The Mongol warriors had traveled deep behind enemy lines. They were ready to attack.

The Shah's soldiers rushed out of the city gates, only to be destroyed. The citizens surrendered without fighting. The Mongols took the city's riches and forced the citizens to come with them. The Mongols forced male prisoners to join the Mongol army. Captured women and children became slaves. The grand city was then burned to the ground.

A HUGE EMPIRE

The Mongols were brutal warriors. When they attacked, they wanted more than riches. They wanted to take control of the land.

In the 1200s, much of eastern Europe and Asia were made up of small kingdoms. Wandering tribes lived on the northern plains of China. They moved around to find better land for their herds of cattle. The Mongol people made up one of these tribes. Mongols were experts with bows and arrows. Warfare was their way of life.

Mongol Genghis Khan came to power in 1206 and united the wandering tribes. Together, they attacked the rich cities of China. They then moved toward the Middle East and eastern Europe. Eventually, the Mongols ruled an empire stretching from Russia to Korea. Mongolia was once the largest connected land empire in world history.

EDGE FACT

Genghis Khan's real name was Temüjin. After becoming the Mongol leader, he changed it to Genghis Khan, meaning "supreme ruler."

Genghis Khan's birthdate is unknown. He was born in either 1162 or 1167.

FIERCE CONQUERORS

The Mongols left a trail of destruction as they traveled. Their soldiers approached cities on horseback. They attacked savagely. Mongol soldiers killed the entire population of some cities. Once inside a city, they took its riches. Many times, they burned everything in a city.

In addition to being great warriors, Mongols were skilled horsemen.

When the Mongols came to a city surrounded by walls, they were patient. They would not let anything come into or out of the city. This battle plan was called laying siege. Citizens only had the food and water that was within the city's walls. Once they ran out of supplies, the citizens either died or surrendered to the Mongols.

CLEVER TACTICS

Genghis Khan used spies on horseback to get information to his generals. Mongol spies found out how cities were protected, how many people lived there, and what type of armies they had. Spies also learned the best route for getting to the cities unnoticed. Using these routes, the Mongols could deliver surprise attacks.

The Mongols also used tricks to fool their enemies. They placed dummies on horseback to make their army look larger. They tied tree branches to the tails of their horses to whip up the dust. The dust clouds made it difficult for their enemies to tell how many soldiers they had. It also made them nearly impossible to follow.

The Mongols also spread stories to scare their enemies. One story tells of a cruel attack that probably never took place. According to the story, the Mongols agreed to leave one particular city. But they made the citizens hand over their pet cats and birds. The people gave up their pets. The Mongols then tied burning torches to the animals' tails and released them. The pets returned to their homes and set the buildings on fire.

Survivors of Mongol attacks were driven out of their cities. They often watched their cities burn to the ground.

CHAPTER II
MONGOL LIFE

When Mongol warriors were not fighting,
they worked as farmers or craftsmen.

LEARN ABOUT:

- *Mongol soldiers*
- *Learning to fight*
- *Paying the khan*

All Mongol men, except doctors, undertakers, and priests, were warriors. The army fought in winter. The rest of the year, Mongols lived in small groups. They cared for their animals and planted crops. When soldiers were needed, each group of Mongols sent men to fight.

The soldiers were not paid, but they did not come home empty-handed. After winning a battle, the Mongols took what they wanted from a city. The goods were divided between the warriors.

Today, many statues honor Genghis Khan.

LIFE UNDER THE KHAN

The khan ruled the Mongol people. The Mongols paid the khan in the form of horses, cows, and sheep. Lords controlled smaller pieces of land under the khan. The Mongols looked after their lord's herds and did chores for him.

Families lived in tents called yurts. The round yurts had a wooden frame covered by felt. These homes were easy to take down when people moved.

Animals played a large role in Mongols' daily life. The people had herds of cows and sheep. They rode horses and hunted rabbits, wild boars, and deer. The Mongols ate the meat and used the animal skins for clothing.

EDGE FACT

Soldiers' families sometimes went with the army. Families traveled behind the main army with the herds of animals the army kept for food.

Both boys and girls studied the world around them. They learned about the land, weather, and animals. Some children learned to read and write. Women cooked, milked livestock, made felt, and sewed. Men focused on hunting and getting ready for war. They made bows and arrows and herded animals.

YOUNG WARRIORS

Mongol boys were raised to be warriors. Many of the games boys played helped them become good soldiers. They began riding horses at 2 or 3 years old and shot small bows and arrows.

The boys learned battle tactics through hunting. They would form a large circle to capture and kill wild game. This exercise taught them how to work together and follow directions.

Eventually, boys learned to shoot a bow and arrow while riding a horse at full gallop.

CHAPTER III

DEADLY WEAPONS

LEARN ABOUT:

- Compound bows
- Combat on horseback
- Waves of warriors

Mongol warriors carried battle axes, curved swords, lances, and compound bows and arrows.

Mongol warriors attacked with bows and arrows. The compound bow was their most valued weapon. It was made from wood and a sheep's horn. An arrow shot from the bow could travel hundreds of yards. The arrow hit its target with deadly force.

Mongols used different types of arrows. Whistling arrows howled through the air. The noise frightened their enemies. Double-sided arrows badly wounded enemies. Mongols shot flaming arrows into cities, setting fire to wooden homes.

MOUNTED WARRIORS

Each Mongol warrior had four or five horses. These valuable animals carried soldiers, weapons, and supplies. Most Mongol warriors attacked from horseback. From a distance, they shot showers of arrows. Up close, they fought hand-to-hand while riding.

Sword
Warriors on horseback carried a sword called a saber.

Helmet
Warriors wore helmets made of iron or leather.

Undershirt
Mongol undershirts were made of strong silk that arrows couldn't rip through.

Horse
Mongol warriors rode small, sturdy ponies.

All warriors carried a small wicker shield covered with leather for protection. Some warriors could not afford armor. But wealthy soldiers wore light armor. The armor included a metal headpiece with cloth flaps covering the ears and neck. Some warriors also wore coats with layers of leather or metal scales. The coats protected the warriors from arrows and other weapons, while allowing them to move easily.

Warriors in the cavalry carried curved swords called sabers and long spears called lances. Poorer soldiers used clubs in close combat.

TACTICS

The Mongol army was often smaller than the forces it faced. Its weapons were no better than those of its enemies. The Mongols won battles because of their military planning.

The first wave of Mongol warriors attacked quickly. Usually, the enemy would chase them. This action led the enemy right into an ambush. There, Mongol warriors on horseback would attack with sabers and lances.

Sometimes, Mongol warriors attacked and quickly retreated. They purposely left equipment and supplies behind. When enemy soldiers came after the goods, the Mongols attacked again.

Some soldiers were experts in siege warfare. They knew how to attack a walled city. Some cities were surrounded by a moat filled with water. Siege engineers taught Mongol warriors how to use catapults, storming ladders, and shields. Catapults sent stones, flaming liquids, and other items over a city's walls. The soldiers climbed over the walls on tall storming ladders. Soldiers hid under gigantic shields as they moved toward a city's walls. Then they filled moats with sandbags and walked across them.

EDGE FACT

The Mongols often spared the lives of craftsmen in a city. The Mongols forced these skilled workers to create weapons, stirrups, and other goods.

During a siege, armed Mongol warriors waited outside the city for their enemies.

CHAPTER IV

DECLINE OF AN EMPIRE

LEARN ABOUT=

- Jealousy
- Defeat
- Local loyalty

At its peak, the Mongol Empire stretched across the entire continent of Asia and into eastern Europe.

The Mongols conquered a large area. But they were better at fighting battles than they were at running a government. After Genghis Khan died, his son Ögodei became the khan. Genghis Khan's other sons and later his grandsons also controlled parts of the empire. As the Mongol Empire spread out, it became difficult to keep together. The leaders in different parts of the empire began to look out for themselves.

FADING POWER

In 1241, the Mongols invaded Poland and Hungary in eastern Europe. But they retreated when they learned Ögodei Khan had died. The soldiers returned to Mongolia to elect a new khan. The Mongol leaders after Ögodei did not push into western Europe.

In the late 1200s, the Mongols began to lose power. Their forces in Syria were defeated by the Mamluks of Egypt. An invasion of Japan failed when strong winds blew the Mongol ships off course.

The Japanese called the wind that kept the Mongols at bay "kamikaze," meaning "divine wind."

Eventually, conflicts arose between leaders in different parts of the empire. Kublai Khan, a grandson of Genghis Khan, ruled China. But he didn't travel with his armies. Without one strong leader, the leaders of the Mongol armies became jealous of each other. They fought among themselves for power. While the Mongols weren't paying attention, countries such as Russia and Manchuria grew powerful. By the end of the 1300s, the Mongol Empire had fallen apart.

The Hazara people of the Middle East are descendants of the Mongols who once conquered that area.

LOSING IDENTITY

Some Mongols lived in the countries they had conquered. They were outnumbered by native people. They lost their Mongolian identity as they adopted local customs, religions, and languages. They became loyal to their local leaders rather than to the leader of Mongolia.

A Chinese saying told to Kublai Khan was, "One can conquer the world on horseback. One cannot govern it on horseback."

Relatives of Genghis Khan ruled in some parts of the empire for hundreds of years, but the Mongol empire was scattered. There was no khan holding power and leading a strong army. The attacks by the fierce warriors on horseback had come to an end.

GLOSSARY

catapult (KAT-uh-puhlt) — a weapon used to hurl rocks, liquid, or other items at an enemy

cavalry (KAV-uhl-ree) — soldiers who travel and fight on horseback

empire (EM-pyr) — a large territory ruled by a powerful leader

khan (KAHN) — the ruler of the Mongols

moat (MOHT) — a deep, wide ditch dug all around a castle, fort, or town and filled with water to prevent attacks

quiver (KWIV-or) — a case for holding arrows

siege (SEEJ) — to surround a city and keep goods and people from going in or out

undertaker (UHN-dur-tay-kur) — someone whose job is to arrange funerals and prepare dead bodies to be buried or cremated

yurt (YURT) — a round tent made of animal skins or felt used as a home by people living in Mongolia

READ MORE

Kent, Zachary. *Genghis Khan: Invincible Ruler of the Mongol Empire.* Rulers of the Middle Ages. Berkeley Heights, N.J.: Enslow, 2008.

Turnbull, Stephen R. *Genghis Khan & the Mongol Conquests, 1190-1400.* Essential Histories. New York: Routledge, 2004.

Whiting, Jim. *The Life and Times of Genghis Khan.* Biography From Ancient Civilizations. Hockessin, Del.: Mitchell Lane, 2005.

INTERNET SITES

FactHound offers a safe, fun way to find Internet sites related to this book. All of the sites on FactHound have been researched by our staff.

Here's how:
1. Visit *www.facthound.com*
2. Choose your grade level.
3. Type in this book ID **1429613122** for age-appropriate sites. You may also browse subjects by clicking on letters, or by clicking on pictures and words.
4. Click on the **Fetch It** button.

FactHound will fetch the best sites for you!

INDEX